Shrinking
Sam

To Ali and Jules (who used to think he would
fall down the drain!) — M. L.

Barefoot Books
124 Walcot Street
Bath BA1 5BG

This book has been printed on 100% acid-free paper

Graphic design by Judy Linard, London
Colour separation by Grafiscan, Verona
Printed and bound in China by Printplus Ltd

This book was typeset in Zemke Hand ITC
The illustrations were prepared in acrylics and collage

Paperback ISBN 978-1-84686-395-0

British Cataloguing-in-Publication Data:
a catalogue record for this book is available from the
British Library

1 3 5 7 9 8 6 4 2

Shrinking
Sam

Written and illustrated by
Miriam Latimer

Barefoot Books
Celebrating Art and Story

'Mum, I think I'm shrinking,' said Sam.
'I couldn't reach my breakfast this morning,
and now I can't reach my coat, and I'm
DEFINITELY not as tall as yesterday.'

'Mmm, lovely, darling,' said Mum. 'Now get ready for school, or you'll miss the bus again.'

By the time Sam had got to school,
he was sure he had shrunk even more.
'Where's your reading book, Sam?'
asked Mrs Barratt.
'Mrs Barratt, I've shrunk so small,
my pencil is the size of a crocodile,
and I think it's trying to
eat me.'

Mrs Barratt sent Sam home with a note.
'Sam is getting too big for his boots.
NO MORE NONSENSE,' she wrote.

At dinnertime, the peas on Sam's plate were so BIG, just one of them filled his whole tummy.

'Dad, I'm definitely shrinking. I'm as small as a tomato. Pete, I'm knee-high to a grasshopper!'

'Mum, Sam's throwing peas at me
again!' Pete said.
'Go and have a bath, Sam, and leave
your brother alone,' said Mum.

Sam slid down to the floor and
climbed into the flowerpot.
Kimba the dog bounded over.
He seemed like a giant.

'Kimba, I'm shrinking.
What am I going to do?
Oh no, Kimba, don't . . .'

'Ahh, Ahhhhh, Ahhhhhhh . . .

. . . Choooo!'
Kimba gave an enormous sneeze, and Sam,
who was now as light as a feather, floated
all the way up to the top of the stairs.

But the bath was far too big for Sam.
So he climbed up the side of a towel
and played in the sink.
'Why doesn't anyone listen
to me?' he shouted.

'I'm shrinking away to nothing!'

As Sam washed, the water
began to swirl around. Faster
and faster it swirled, and as it
swirled it dropped lower and
lower. The plug had come out!

'Oh no!' Sam cried, as he felt himself being sucked down the plughole.
'HELP!'

Sam whooshed down the drain. His heart was thumping, and he was sure he was going to drown.

As the drain grew darker and colder,
he began to shiver.
'I—i—is anyone there?' he stuttered.
He was shivering all over and his teeth
were chattering.
'I—i—is anyone there?' his voice echoed
back. Sam began to cry.

'Quick! Grab hold of this!' came a small voice, and Sam felt himself being pulled up on to a floating sponge.
'Who are you?' he asked, staring at the small girl on top of the sponge.

'I'm Izzy,' she replied cheerfully. 'This happens to me all the time. I shrink every time my family ignores me. Today, I shrank so much that I fell down the toilet. Why are you so small?'

'The same thing happened to me, but I fell down the sink,' explained Sam, staring at her. As the two children shared their stories, they started to grow a bit, and as they listened to each other, they grew a bit more.

'Hooray, I'm starting to grow!' cried Sam.
'And so are you!'
Izzy just smiled. 'Come on,' she said.
'We need to start paddling.'

'I can see a light ahead,'
called Izzy. 'I think it's your
home.'
'What about you?' asked Sam.
'Don't worry. The next stop's
my house.'

'Bye, Izzy, and thank you.' Sam leapt off the sponge and into the light. He landed with a thump in a pile of damp clothes.

'Those are my pyjamas, and that's Amy's tee-shirt . . . I know where I am. I'm inside the washing machine! But how am I going to get out?'

'Woof!' barked Kimba from outside, and he bounded over, wagging his tail. He opened the door with his paw, and gave Sam a BIG lick. Sam felt himself grow a little bit bigger.

'Sam!' gurgled his baby sister.
'Wow, you've learnt to say my name!'

Amy blew him a kiss through the air, and Sam felt himself grow even bigger.

'Hello, Sam!' said Dad. 'Have you had your bath?' asked Mum. 'We wondered what you were up to. We thought you might have fallen down the plughole!'

Sam grinned as Mum and Dad gave him a BIG LONG hug . . .

... and he felt himself grow even bigger than before! 'I'm starving!' he said. 'Is there anything to eat?'